DINO-SOCCER

Lisa Wheeler
Illustrations by Barry Gott

 CAROLRHODA BOOKS MINNEAPOLIS · NEW YORK

To Aunt Betty
and all her grandkids.
Love, L.W.

For Rose, Finn, and Nandi
—B.G.

Text copyright © 2009 by Lisa Wheeler
Illustrations copyright © 2009 by Barry Gott

Carolrhoda Books
A division of Lerner Publishing Group, Inc.
241 First Avenue North
Minneapolis, MN 55401 U.S.A.

Website address: www.lernerbooks.com

Library of Congress Cataloging-in-Publication Data

Wheeler, Lisa, 1963-
     Dino-soccer / by Lisa Wheeler ; illustrated by Barry Gott.
        p.   cm.
     Summary: Plant-eating dinosaurs face meat-eating dinosaurs in a
soccer match.
     ISBN 978-0-8225-9028-6 (lib. bdg. : alk. paper)
     [1. Stories in rhyme. 2. Dinosaurs—Fiction. 3. Soccer—Fiction.]
I. Gott, Barry, ill. II. Title.

PZ8.3.W5668Din 2009
[E]—dc22   2008039197

Manufactured in the United States of America
1 2 3 4 5 6 - DP - 14 13 12 11 10 09

Dinos huddle up at noon.
Soccer game is starting soon.

Here come herds of soccer fans
and dino-moms in minivans.

Locker Room

Decked in colors, proud and bold—
BITERS blue and GRAZERS gold.

Their uniforms are loose and bright.
Their socks hold shin guards nice
and tight.

BITERS
T. REX —STRIKER
PTERODACTYL TWINS—WINGERS
GALLIMIMUS—MIDFIELDER
COMPSOGNATHUS—MIDFIELDER
RAPTOR—DEFENSEMAN
ALLOSAURUS—DEFENSEMAN
TROODON—GOALIE

GRAZERS
ANKYLOSAURUS—STRIKER
LESOTHOSAURUS—WINGER
TRICERATOPS—WINGER
DIPLODOCUS—MIDFIELDER
APATOSAURUS—MIDFIELDER
STEGOSAURUS—DEFENSEMAN
PACHYCEPHALOSAUR—DEFENSEMAN
IGUANODON—GOALIE

Leso traps it with his feet.
Although he's small,
his moves are sweet.

He zigs. He zags.
He scampers 'round.
The two defenders
stand their ground.

Time to warm up legs and tails.
Bend those legs, and stretch those scales!

The ref jogs in to do his part.
A coin is tossed. The Grazers start.

Ankylosaurus makes the pass,
a sneaky side kick through the grass.

A pass to Diplo—off he goes!

He sneaks the ball past goalie toes.

He makes the first point of the day.
The Grazers fans shout "Hip-hooray!"

A quick reset. No time to stall.
Biters' turn to move the ball.

T. rex travels, yard by yard,
then Stegosaurus checks him hard.

Side by side 'til **Stego** steals.
Watch out! Two wingers on his heels.

With wicked wings and clever claws,
the **Pterodactyls** take the ball.

One winger makes an outside shot.
There's **Gallimimus** on the spot.

Then **Galli** takes it to the net.
Score! This game's not over yet.

Her soccer cleats have lost their tread,
but Pachy likes to use her head!

The ball goes up. Tricera spikes it.

The ball deflates . . . and no one likes it.

The Grazers seem to be in charge.
Apatosaur is looming large.

The ball sails through the goalie's hands.
The fans go crazy in the stands.

They love their teams. They're having fun.
It's Grazers—2 and Biters—1.

T. rex attacks. He's on the move.
A pass to **Raptor**, nice and smooth.

Little **Leso**, light and small—
a shoulder charge! He steals the ball.

He dribbles left. He dribbles right.
Compy tackles—dino fight!

Both players get a penalty.
Red cards from the referee.

The **Biters** whine. The **Grazers** pout
as both the brawlers sit it OUT.

The **Pterodactyl** twins advance toward Grazers' goal. They see their chance.

Pass to **Allo**. Comin' through!
A perfect shot! It's 2 to 2.

Here comes **Galli!** Quick and sure,
she weaves between each dinosaur.

Gallimimus kicks it fast.
Iguano's grazing on the grass!

The gold fans groan and stomp and roar.
Iguano goofed! The Biters score!

As Grazers spirits all deflate, the winning Biters celebrate!

They wave their flags and roar with glee.
They end the year with victory!

But wait and see...

Get your tickets, one and all!
Next season, they'll play **Dino-ball!**